Georgiana

Algernon Hall

A story for children.

Georgiana

Algernon Hall
A story for children

ISBN/EAN: 9783337218331

Printed in Europe, USA, Canada, Australia, Japan

Cover: Foto ©Andreas Hilbeck / pixelio.de

More available books at **www.hansebooks.com**

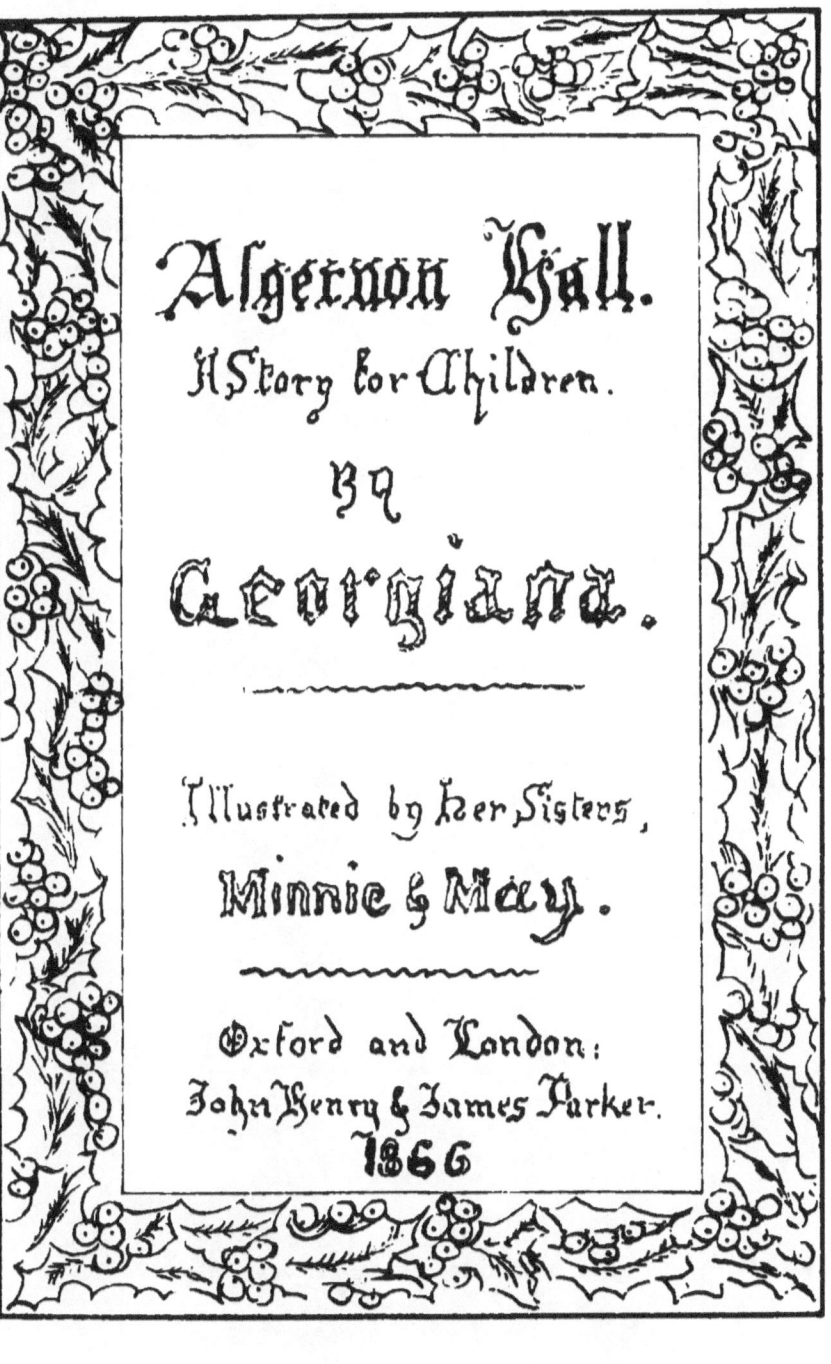

Algernon Hall.

A Story for Children.

By

Georgiana.

Illustrated by her Sisters,

Minnie & May.

Oxford and London:

John Henry & James Parker.

1866

TO

My Mother,

FROM WHOSE DEAR LIPS I LEARNT MY FIRST LESSON

OF OBEDIENCE,

I DEDICATE THIS LITTLE BOOK,

IN TOKEN THAT HER WORDS HAVE NOT BEEN FOR-

GOTTEN BY HER AFFECTIONATE CHILD,

GEORGIANA.

PREFACE.

"CAST thy bread upon the waters : for thou shalt find it after many days."

So, gentle reader, is this little book sent forth in its gay and glittering colours, to assist a poor and helpless cripple, to obtain an asylum where he may repose in rest and quiet, till such time as God has appointed him.

Many of our celebrated authors think it well to say a few words to the reader by way of introduction, and I would fain profit by their example ; for indeed there is great need for me to ask the readers of the following little story to shew clemency in their perusal of it.

"Algernon Hall" was written by a little girl of thirteen years of age during her holidays : it was written in secret, whilst the other children (for Georgiana is one of a large family of merry urchins) amused themselves in various ways, as children do when studies are set aside, and the long looked-for holidays have at length arrived. Day by day the little maiden stole away to her hiding-place, and there noted down the incidents which are related in the tale ; and when the whole was completed, and not till then, the book (made of scribbling paper neatly stitched into a most original brown paper cover) was presented to the eldest sister of the family, with a request that if she thought it "good enough," it might be given to "dear mamma."

The illustrations are by Georgiana's sisters, girls of fourteen and fifteen years of age.

The story is a trifle in itself, and would certainly never have appeared in the gay dress it now wears had it not been for the earnest entreaties of the little girl that the book might be sold to help a poor sufferer—the son of an old servant of the family—in his endeavours to gain admission into the Royal Hospital for Incurables.

Any indication of a wish to alleviate the sufferings of others, any desire (however feebly expressed) to be of use in their generation, any shewing forth of an anxiety to follow in the footsteps of our dear Lord and Master in their children, must cause the hearts of parents to overflow with gratitude for the goodness of

God in thus early implanting the heavenly seed in the hearts of their little ones.

That the poor cripple may find a home for life through the ministrations of a child, that other children in reading the following little story may benefit by the lesson of obedience, and may be induced to exert themselves to help their fellow-creatures, and that Georgiana may not rest satisfied with one effort at doing good, but may continue to grow in grace, are amongst the heartfelt desires of

HER MOTHER.

ALGERNON HALL.

CHAPTER I.

"YOU are a naughty, cross boy, Charlie ; you're always teasing one !"

Such was the exclamation uttered by a little girl of apparently twelve years of age. A boy two years younger was standing at her side, amusing himself by picking off the heads of her flowers : wearied at last with begging him not to do so, the poor child ran away, completely out of patience. She had hardly been gone five minutes when the eldest of the family was seen approaching the boy ; she was tall, pretty, and about fourteen years of age ; so like Charlie that any one might have recognised her as his sister.

" Where is Annie ?" she exclaimed.

" She has run away, and is horribly cross, as usual."

" You've been teasing her again, Charlie ; it is very unkind of you, when Mamma has told you so many times not to do so. You know how delicate she is—but hark ! the clock is striking five, and tea will be ready. Run in, while I go and fetch Annie."

The boy moved away, but made no response, and Alice ran to look for her sister, whom she found sitting under her favourite tree, reading.

" Come, Annie dear, make haste and come in to tea, for the clock has struck, and we shall be late."

So saying, the two girls proceeded towards the house. They entered a pleasant, cheerful-looking room, where Charlie and Miss Hill, the governess, were sitting at the tea-table.

" You must not be late again, Alice," said Miss Hill, " or I shall be obliged to punish you."

The two girls sat down, and while they are drinking their tea I will give my readers some idea of this family, before proceeding farther with my story.

Mr. and Mrs. Hood had married when very young. Mrs. Hood was an only child : her mother had died when she was an infant, and she had been brought up by her father, who was a very old man. Mr. Hood had seen her for the first time at a ball given in their neigh-bourhood. He fell in love with her,

and they were married just before her
father died.   After the funeral they went
abroad for five years, and at last settled
down at Algernon Hall, with their three
children, Alice, Annie, and Charlie.

Algernon Hall is a fine old mansion,
situated in one of the most picturesque
and romantic spots of Derbyshire.   It
abounds in beautiful woods, gardens,
grounds, and walks.   The estate be-
longed to Mr. Hood at the time of my
story, and was considered one of the
finest for miles round, and was much
visited by artists, tourists, &c.

Such was the history and residence
of this family at the commencement of
my story.

CHAPTER II

CHAPTER II.

" ANNIE," cried Alice, rushing into the school-room one bright summer morning, "what do you think Mamma has just told me? You know Miss Hill is going home for her holidays next week; well, we are all to go to the sea-side for a fortnight, so that you may get quite strong again."

"What fun! what fun!" cried Annie. "When are we going?"

"On Monday week," said Alice; "but I must be off and tell Charlie." So saying, away she ran.

The children were very excited about their treat, and when Sunday night arrived, they could hardly be persuaded to go to bed.

" I do so hope it will be fine," said Annie to Alice.

" Yes," Alice replied ; " call me if you are awake first."

" Very well," was the reply, and the children were soon asleep.

Monday morning dawned. A mist hung over the hills, the cattle were lowing, and the little birds were singing their morning song of thanksgiving to their Maker, who made all things so beautiful.

Annie awoke, jumped out of her bed, and threw open her window. The fresh air fanned her warm cheeks as she looked out. Having satisfied herself that it was a fine day, she awoke Alice. They were soon dressed, and

without loss of time joined their brother, who was already in the garden. It was very warm even then, though it was not more than seven o'clock. Having said " Good-bye" to all their pets, they then returned to the house for breakfast, and at nine o'clock they drove to the railway station, which they reached just in time.

At Oakham Station, Miss Hill had to leave them, as her home lay in a different direction. The journey was a long one, and the children were getting very tired, so their mamma proposed they should go to sleep; they wisely acted upon her advice, and slept until their papa said, " Look at the sea, children."

The calm and beautiful water lay stretched in all its beauty before their eyes, the rippling waves sounding refreshing.

The railway was close to the shore, so they could see the little children digging in the sand as they passed along; Alice, Annie and Charlie, had only been to the sea-side once before, and that was when they were quite little children, and their delight was very great, when they found that the hotel in which they were to lodge was opposite the sea.

After their tea their mamma took them down to the shore for a little walk, and it was very late before they were in bed, dreaming of the many happy days they were to spend at St. Edric.

CHAPTER III

CHAPTER III.

SEVERAL weeks had passed away
since the arrival of the Hoods at
St. Edric. The children had enjoyed
themselves exceedingly. Their parents
had arranged several picnics and boat-
ing expeditions for them : but the sea-
bathing was their especial delight; they
learnt how to swim and float, and Charlie
to row and dive. But it is not my in-
tention to record what happened every
day, only one event, which made an im-
pression on the minds of the children,
and will shew my young readers the
effects of disobedience.

It was a lovely morning a short time

before their departure from St. Edric, when Annie and Charlie came up to Mrs. Hood, who was sitting with Alice on the beach reading, and asked permission to go round the point that Charlie might pick up some agates, which they had been told abounded there.

"You may go, children," replied Mrs. Hood, "on condition you do not go beyond the cliff; and remember, Annie, you are the eldest, as Alice will remain with me : therefore be careful, and mind what I have told you."

They promised to be very good, and ran away : the children did not find as many agates as they had anticipated, but Charlie soon espied some beautiful shells.

"Oh Annie, never mind the agates,"

said the boy; " see, there are some lovely shells."

" But, Charlie," said Annie, " the shells are on the other side of the cliff, where you know Mamma told us not to go; come, Charlie, come away, we must not go there."

"Oh, nonsense," said the boy, " it does not matter; it is only *just* round the point; there's nothing to hurt us : come along, Annie, and don't be so silly." Annie stood undecided; another minute, and she had followed her brother. Ah, if those children could only have known the result, and danger of disobedience, they surely could not have so soon forgotten the words of their dear mother; how little did either of them imagine the danger into which they were both running! But to return to the children :

c

they stayed so long picking up the
shells, and sorting the sea-weeds, that
neither of them perceived the tide
had turned, and was rapidly approaching them; it had turned the point, indeed, before either of them looked up,
so intent were they on their pursuit. It
was of no use for them to try and es-
cape now, for behind them rose a tall
perpendicular rock, which would have
been as difficult to climb as the walls
of a room; before them, and on one
side, lay the boundless ocean, and on
the only side remaining, the point of
which they had turned, were the cliffs
which no human being could scale.
Their terror was extreme; the thought
of such a slow terrible death, the re-
membrance of their disobedience, and
that they might never see their parents

again, all rushed across their minds. Oh,
what would they not have given never
to have disobeyed, then they would
have been safe on the beach instead
of on this awful spot: many times
Annie and Charlie resolved never to
be disobedient again, if it might only
please God, to spare them this once.
The sun was hidden behind the clouds,
the tall crested waves rose higher and
higher, the sea-gulls flitted here and
there; not a boat, not a human being,
was to be seen : oh that they had not
disobeyed.

"Annie, dear Annie," said the boy,
"look at the angry waves, how they dash
in; surely each one comes nearer to us
than the last. Oh Annie, dear Annie!"
repeated the poor little boy, "we shall
be drowned, indeed we shall; there is

nobody to help us, and we shall never
see Papa, and Mamma, and Alice, any
more, and God will surely punish us
for being so naughty."

Higher and higher rose the great, tall
waves; in ten minutes it would be too
late to try and save them. Then they
remembered that when no human hand
can save, there is One who is ever
ready to listen, and help. They knelt,
and prayed for forgiveness for their
sins; through the roaring waves and
wind the prayer ascended to heaven,
and was heard, and answered.

At last, Annie, overcome with fatigue,
terror, and anxiety, fell fainting to the
ground. Charlie seized her by the hand
and drew her higher to the rock; he
leant over the poor little girl, and said,
" Annie, oh Annie, speak to me, do

speak to me." But no answer was returned. Thus he remained some little
time; and now he began to feel that
if help did not very soon come, they
must die, for every moment brought
the waves nearer, and they could go
no farther back; his hand was so be-
numbed with cold that he could hardly
hold Annie any longer; but still he
trusted with childlike faith in Him to
whom they had prayed for mercy. At
last, half despairing of ever being rescued from their horrible situation, he
raised his eyes once more to heaven, when he saw something upon the
waters—a boat! a boat upon the stormy
sea! He called, he shouted, and waved
his handkerchief; one moment of in-
tense anxiety, and to his unutterable joy
he saw the boat turn towards them. He

leant over his sister : " Dearest Annie, help is coming," said the loving brother, even though Annie heard him not. The little craft quickly made its way, and soon approached them ; the good fisherman stretched forth his arms and placed the wanderers in safety in the boat.

They were safe ; their prayer was heard, and they were rescued !

CHAPTER IV

CHAPTER IV.

BUT we must now leave Annie and Charlie for a little while, and return to Mrs. Hood and Alice. An hour had passed since the children had left them, and they were getting anxious; when Mr. Hood returning from his walk asked for Annie and Charlie, his wife explained to him what had taken place during his absence, adding that she was feeling anxious about the children. Mr. Hood immediately retraced his steps to the cottage of an old fisherman, where he learnt to his horror that the tide must have covered the rock already; but the old man said he would take a boat and go and see what could be done. The boat was put off, and having seen it start, Mr. Hood returned to his wife and daughter, hoping perhaps to find his little ones already by their mother's side. Alas! nothing had been heard of the children. Soon, however, the anxious parents and their eldest girl perceived a boat making for the shore. Mr. Hood ran down to see if the occupants knew anything about his dear children : what was his joy and surprise to see his darlings in that boat! The fisherman told Mr. Hood how he had found the children, and Mrs. Hood and Alice were soon at the water's edge, embracing the loved ones, and hearing the old fisherman's wondrous story.

Annie was still too faint and ill to tell what had befallen them ; but ere the

children closed their eyes that night, they begged to be forgiven their act of disobedience. A serious illness followed this sad day. Annie, always a delicate child, was attacked with low fever, from which it was for some time feared that she might not recover.

Sadly the days passed by. At length the crisis was over, and Annie was out of danger. Her recovery was now rapid, but the effects of disobedience were not effaced from the minds of Charlie and Annie. When tempted to disobey their parents they remembered St. Edric, and how nearly they had lost their lives by a single act of disobedience.

A FEW words of thanks before we part, dear Readers, a few words of gratitude from those who are indeed truly

sensible of the kindness of the Subscribers to this little Book. It speaks
well for the love of charity in this land,
that no sooner was the object for which
" Algernon Hall" was to be published
made known in a necessarily limited
circle, than above one thousand copies
of the Work were subscribed for. " Many
can help one" is an old adage; and we
trust, with God's blessing, that all who
have so kindly added their support to
Georgiana's first literary effort may know,
ere long, that an asylum for life has
been found for the poor suffering cripple
whom it hath pleased God to afflict so
heavily : for the Incurable that we are
labouring for does not ask for a pension ;
he has *no home* to take money to ; it is
for admission into the Hospital that he
entreats so earnestly, for a place of refuge

where he can repose for the remainder of his days upon earth.

Should success be attained, and the sufferer be placed among the candidates who have been elected for admission into the Royal Hospital for Incurables, the Subscribers to this little Work will once more hear from the juvenile workers. Till then, dear Readers, with heartfelt gratitude, we bid you all adieu.

LIST OF SUBSCRIBERS.

THE LORD ARCHBISHOP OF CANTERBURY, 5 *copies.*

The Lord Archbishop of Dublin, 6 copies

	Copies		Copies
Marchioness of Aylesbury	10	Lord Bishop of Oxford .	2
Earl of Suffolk . .	1	Lord Bishop of Chichester	10
Dowager Countess of Bel-		Lord Bishop of Peterborough	2
more	1	Lord Bishop of Edinburgh	2
Countess of Clancarty .	1	Lady Willoughby de Broke	5
Earl of Effingham . .	1	Baroness Sempill . .	1
Countess of Effingham .	1	Lord Sherborne . .	5
Dowager Viscountess Sid-		Lady Sherborne . .	5
mouth . . .	5	Lady Braybrooke . .	2
Viscount Andover . .	1	Lady Gifford . . .	1
Lady Isabel Atherley .	1	Lady de Mauley . .	1
Lady Elizabeth Leslie Mel-		Baroness de Teissier .	1
ville Cartwright . .	3	Hon. and Rev. G. Talbot	1
Lady Lavinia Dutton .	1	Hon. Mrs. Gustavus Talbot	1
Lady Laura Palmer . .	1	Hon. and Rev. F. Bertie .	1
Lady Frances B. Simpson	1	Hon. Mrs. A. G. Douglas	6
Lady Georgina Bathurst .	1	Hon. William Bathurst .	3
Lady Emily Ponsonby .	1	Hon. Mrs. P. S. Pierrepont	1
Lady Catherine Wheble .	1	Hon. Percy Barrington .	1
Lady Georgina Bertie .	1	Hon. Mrs. P. Barrington .	1
Lady Emily McNaghten .	1	Hon. Margaret Verney .	5
Lady Louisa S. Harrison .	3	Hon. and Rev. T. W. Fiennes	1
Lady Louisa Le Poer Trench	1	Hon. Mrs. T. W. Fiennes	1
Lady Harriet Kavanagh .	1	Hon. Mrs. Palmer-More-	
Lady Mary Frances Egerton	1	wood	4
Lady Georgiana Fullerton	5	Hon. Frances Rice . .	1
Lady Katharine Raymond-		Hon. Maria Rice . .	2
Barker . . .	1	Hon. Mrs. Wrighton .	2
Lady John Chichester .	1	Hon. Julia Dutton . .	1
Lady Augustus FitzClarence	1	Hon. Charles Dutton .	2
Lord Bishop of London .	3	Hon. John Dutton . .	1
Lord Bishop of Winchester	10	Hon. Emily Wynn . .	1

	Copies
Hon. and Rev. William Blackwood . . .	2
Hon. Mrs. W. Blackwood	2
Hon. Mrs. Hamilton Ward	1
Hon. Mrs. Gore Browne	2
Hon. Mrs. Hankey . .	1
Hon. and Rev. C. Spencer	1
Hon. Mrs. Chas. Spencer	3
Hon. Mrs. Allen Bathurst	1
Hon. Ashley Ponsonby .	1
Hon. Mrs. Ashley Ponsonby	1
Hon. and Rev. E. Wrottesley	3
Hon. Mrs. E. Wrottesley	2
Hon. Alfred Thesiger .	1
Hon. Mrs. Alfred Thesiger	1
Hon. Lady Talbot . .	1
Hon. Mrs. Wodehouse Currie	1
A Soldier's Mother . .	10
Lady Shelley of Manesfield	1
Sir M. Hicks Beach, Bt., M.P.	1
Dowager Lady Hicks Beach	1
Lady Isham . . .	5
Lady Carmichael Anstruther	1
Lady Chetwode . .	5
Sir Henry Bromley, Bart.	1
Lady Bromley . . .	2
Dowager Lady Bromley .	1
Lady Carmichael Smyth .	1
Sir Velters Cornewall, Bt.	1
Sir Maxwell Steele Graves, Bt.	1
Lady Steele Graves . .	1
Capt. Sir Algernon Peyton, Bt.	5
Rev. Sir Henry Gunning, Bt.	2
Lady Gunning . . .	2
Sir William Guise, Bart. .	1
Lady Guise . . .	1
Dowager Lady Onslow .	1

	Copies
Dowager Lady Duff Gordon	1
Dowager Lady Cuyler .	1
Sir Thomas Waller, Bart.	3
Sir George Pocock, Bart.	1
Lady Pocock . . .	1
Sir Wm. Russell, Bt., M.P.	2
Lady Russell . . .	2
Rev. Sir E. Armstrong, Bt.	1
Lady Armstrong . .	1
Dowager Lady Armstrong	3
Lady Goldsmid . .	3
Lady Cartwright . .	1
Gen. Sir H. Taylor, K.C.B.	1
Sir G. R. Clerk, K.C.B., S.I.	6
Lady Russell Clerk . .	6
Lady Davy . . .	1
Vice-Chancellor of Oxford	1
Dean of Ch. Ch. . .	1
Archdeacon Clerke . .	4
Master of University Coll.	1
Master of Balliol Coll. .	2
Warden of Merton Coll. .	1
Provost of Oriel Coll. .	1
Provost of Queen's Coll. .	1
Warden of New Coll. .	1
Rector of Lincoln Coll. .	1
Warden of All Souls .	1
President of Magdalen Coll.	1
Principal of Brasenose Coll.	1
President of C.C.C. . .	1
President of Trinity Coll. .	5
Principal of Jesus Coll. .	1
Warden of Wadham Coll.	2
Master of Pembroke Coll.	1
Rev. the Librarian of the Bodleian Library . .	1

DR. ACLAND . . .	1
Mrs. Acland . . .	1
Mrs. Abell . . .	1

Rev. T. Dawson Allen .	1
R. Ackerman, Esq. . .	3
A. Ackerman, Esq. . .	3

	Copies		Copies
Mrs. Allen	1	Miss Beagley	1
Mrs. Andrews	1	Mrs. Beckford	1
Edward Atkinson, Esq.	10	Frank Beckford, Esq.	1
John Arkwright, Esq.	1	Miss Beckford	1
Francis H. Atherley, Esq.	1	Miss Joanna Beckford	1
John Ashhurst, Esq.	1	Miss M. Beckford	1
Mrs. Ashhurst	1	Rev. Joe A. Beckett	1
J. S. Ashley, Esq.	1	Mrs. Beckett	1
Mrs. Apthorpe	1	E. Bevers, Esq.	1
E. C. Austen, Esq.	1	Major Bigge, 5th Fusiliers	2
Mrs. Atkins	1	Lieut.-Col. Bigge	1
Frederick Andrew, Esq.	1	Mrs. Bigge	2
		Robert Blackwood, Esq.	1
Allen Bathurst, Esq., M.P.	1	Mrs. Blood	3
Rev. H. Raymond Barker	1	Lieut.-Col. Bickerstaff	3
Barwick Baker, Esq.	1	Mrs. Bickerstaff	2
Mrs. Barwick Baker	1	Col. Bowyer	1
Rev. Charles Bartholomew	1	Rev. Fitzwilliam Bowyer	1
Mrs. Windham Baring	1	Miss Fanny Bowyer	3
Rev. Chandos Bailey	1	Miss Mary Bowyer	1
Mrs. Chandos Bailey	1	William Barnard	10
J. Barclay, Esq.	5	Miss Boulter	1
Mrs. H. Raymond Barker	1	Rev. William Browning	1
Mrs. Baly	6	Mrs. William Browning	1
Mrs. Bradley	1	Rev. Oscar Browning	1
Miss Bayne	1	Mrs. Browning	1
Mrs. Freeman Bishop	1	Col. Bonamy	1
Miss Barrington	1	Mrs. Bowly	6
Mrs. Braithwaite	1	Rev. J. H. Brookes	1
Charles Bates, Esq.	1	Mrs. Brookes	1
Mrs. Barneby	1	Miss Bradley	1
Mrs. Henry Barnett	2	Mrs. Bingham	2
Major Barnett	3	Miss Bond	1
Mrs. Barclay	2	Mrs. Bolland	1
Mrs. Hicks Beach	1	Mrs. Charles Brown	6
Mrs. Beale	5	General Boyd	1
Miss Bennett	1	Rev. James Bruce	1
Mrs. Head Best	1	Rev. Lloyd Stewart Bruce	3
Mrs. J. N. Benthall	1	Mrs. Bailie	5
Mrs. Richard Lee Bevan	10	Mrs. Bulteel	5
Mrs. Barat	5	Mrs. Butler	1
John Benham, Esq.	5	A. B. Bullock, Esq.	1

	Copies		*Copies*
Rev. William Buckley	1	Mrs. Collins	2
Mrs. William Buckley	1	William Cooke, Esq., Q.C.	1
Mrs. William Bygrave	6	Miss Cooke	1
Mrs. Bulley	1	Mrs. Cooke	1
		Cregoe Colmore, Esq.	3
General Cartwright	5	Mrs. Clerke	2
Col. Cartwright, M.P.	1	Capel Croome, Esq.	2
Rev. Frederick Cartwright	10	Miss Croome	1
Mrs. Henry Cartwright	1	Miss Cranstone	1
Mrs. Cameron	1	G. Wodehouse Currie, Esq.	1
Col. Campbell	1	Rev. James Crosse	1
Mrs. Campbell	1	Miss Croome	6
Miss Lucy Campbell	1	Ellis Cunliffe, Esq.	2
J. Canning, Esq.	1	Miss Cunliffe	2
Lieut.-Col. Chetwode	3	Miss C. Cunliffe	3
Mrs. Augustus Chetwode	2	Capt. Cunliffe	1
Miss Chetwode	6	Miss Crosbie	1
Mrs. Christie	1		
Mrs. Charlton	1	T. Tyrwhitt Drake, Esq.	5
Mrs. Chandler	2	Mrs. Tyrwhitt Drake	5
Mrs. Chester	2	Miss Harriet Drake	1
Mildmay Clerk, Esq.	2	Mrs. T. Daubeny	1
Mrs. Mildmay Clerk	1	J. Davenport, Esq.	1
Miss Cornewall	2	Mrs. Davies	1
Miss Cornish	1	E. Leopold Denys, Esq.	2
Rev. T. H. Cookes	3	Tomkyns Dew, Esq.	2
Mrs. Gascoigne Clare	12	Mrs. Dent, Sudeley Castle	6
Col. Cleather	1	Mrs. Dewar	1
Miss Cleather	1	Rev. H. J. Fane De Salis	1
Mrs. Colley	1	Mrs. De Salis	1
Mrs. Cole	2	Miss De Barnerdy	2
Herbert Clark, Esq.	1	Mrs. Dagley	1
William C. Carbonell, Esq.	1	B. Daniell, Esq.	10
Miss Carbonell	1	Miss Daniell	5
Miss M. Carbonell	1	Miss Blanche Daniell	5
Major Cornwallis	1	Mrs. Drayton	3
Mrs. Cornwallis	1	John Downing, Esq.	3
Mrs. Cooper, Stoke Park	1	Gen. Downing	1
Mrs. Cooper	1	Mrs. Downing	1
Mrs. Cowper	6	Charles Downing, Esq.	2
Mrs. Coker	1	Cameron Downing, Esq.	1
Mrs. Clayton	2	Valentine Durant, Esq.	2

	Copies		Copies
Mrs. Dunn, of Inglefield .	5	Delamark Freeman, Esq. .	1
Miss Dunn, of Inglefield .	5	C. Freebody, Esq. . .	12
— Dunn, Esq., of Inglefield	5	Mrs. Freebourg . .	3
T. Dunn, Esq. . . .	2	Captain Foster . . .	1
Mrs. Dunn . . .	2	Mrs. Foster . . .	1
Mrs. Donne . . .	1	William Foster, Esq. .	3
Mrs. Dixon . . .	1	Mrs. Fortescue . .	2
Mrs. Delolme . . .	10	George Fuller, Esq. .	1
Capt. Donnithorne . .	1	Mrs. George Fuller . .	1
Mrs. Donnithorne . .	1	Alexander Fullerton, Esq.	5
James Dorington, Esq. .	1	David Fullerton, Esq. .	20
Mrs. Dorington . .	1	Mrs. David Fullerton .	10
Mrs. John E. Dorington .	1	Miss Fullerton . . .	3
		Miss Amy Fullerton .	5
Mrs. Ellicott . . .	4	Master D. E. D. Fullerton	2
E. C. Egerton, Esq., M.P.	1	Miss Helen Fullerton .	1
Miss Egerton . . .	1	Miss Emily Fullerton .	1
Mrs. Edgeworth . .	2	Master G. F. D. Fullerton	1
John Henry Elwes, Esq. .	5	Miss C. Violet Fullerton .	1
Mrs. Elwes . . .	2	Miss E. Marianne Fullerton	1
Wynn Ellis, Esq. . .	2	Miss A. Le Poer Fullerton	1
Miss Ellis . . .	2	Mrs. Furse . . .	1
Miss Elwes . . .	1	Rev. James Fyler . .	2
Mrs. Edmunds . .	5		
Mrs. Edmonstone . .	1	Rev. Alfred Gatty, D.D. .	1
N. B. Edmonstone, Esq. .	1	Mrs. Alfred Gatty . .	1
Mrs. Evetts . . .	1	Alfred Scott Gatty, Esq. .	1
H. R. Eyre, Esq. . .	2	Charles Gatty, Esq. . .	1
Mrs. Eyre . . .	1	Henry Gaskell, Esq. .	1
Miss Eyre . . .	1	Mrs. Gaskell . . .	1
		Mrs. Gibbs . . .	1
Mrs. Peter Fairbairn .	1	Mrs. Gibbon . . .	1
Col. Fane, M.P. . .	2	Mrs. Murray Gartshore .	2
Mrs. Fane . . .	2	Miss Duff Gordon . .	1
Mrs. FitzGerald . .	1	Rev. E. M. Goulburn, D.D.	1
Rev. John Fisher, D.D. .	5	Mrs. E. M. Goulburn .	1
J. Finch, Esq. . .	2	C. Goldeney, Esq. . .	1
Miss Finsdon . . .	1	Mrs. Gough . . .	6
Miss Fenwick . . .	1	Mrs. Grassett . . .	5
F. M. Fenwick, Esq. .	1	Harman Grisewood, Esq.	1
H. C. Fenwick, Esq. .	3	H. Grisewood, Esq., Junr.	3
Capt. Hawkins Fisher .	2	Miss Greatrix . . .	1

	Copies		Copies
James Green, Esq. . .	3	Edmund Hopkinson, Esq.	1
Mrs. James Green . .	3	Mrs. Hopkinson . .	1
Mrs. Henry Guise . .	1	Miss Hopkinson . .	1
		Mrs. Holland . . .	3
Mrs. G. Barnard Hankey .	1	Mrs. Houseden . .	1
Miss Barnard Hankey .	1	Miss Howard . . .	1
Charles Hancock, Esq. .	3	Mrs. Hunt . . .	5
Alick Hall, Esq. . .	4	Henry Huth, Esq. . .	5
Mrs. Hall . . .	3	James Hutchinson, Esq. .	5
Mrs. Hands . . .	2		
Mrs. W. Hall . . .	1	Rev. William Ince . .	2
Miss Harris . . .	1	Miss Ilderton . . .	1
Major Hartley . . .	1	Leopold Iverson, Esq. .	1
Mrs. Hartley . . .	1		
J. Hammond, Esq. . .	5	Mrs. Jeune . . .	1
Henry Hall, Esq. . .	1	Mrs. James . . .	1
Mrs. Edmund Harrington	1	G. Ashton Jonson, Esq. .	1
Mrs. Arthur Hastie . .	1	Miss Edith Ashton Jonson	1
Mrs. Finch Hatton . .	1	Frederick Johnson, Esq.,	
Mrs. Hayes . . .	1	H. B. M. Consul, Tampico	1
Mrs. Hetley . . .	1	Rev. Chas. Johnson, Esq.	1
Mrs. Harvey . . .	2	J. Johnson, Esq. . .	10
Mrs. Heel . . .	3	A. Johnson, Esq. . .	2
A. Henderson, Esq. .	2	Mrs. Johnson . . .	2
Rev. Stanley Hill . .	6	J. Jackman, Esq. . .	1
Mrs. Stanley Hill . .	3	Mrs. Jackman . . .	1
Mrs. Hill . . .	8	Mrs. Judd . . .	1
Mrs. T. Hill . . .	2	Miss Johnstone . .	1
Rev. James Hill . .	1	J. R. Kenyon, Esq., D.C.L.,	
Mrs. W. S. Hill . .	1	Vinerian Professor .	1
Miss Hill . . .	3	Rev. A. Kent, M.A. .	1
Miss Hall . . .	1	Mrs. Kent . . .	1
W. Tetlow Hibbert, Esq.	1	John Kemp, Esq. . .	1
Miss Hibbert . . .	1	Col. King, Stratton Hall	12
Col. Hibbert . . .	1	Miss King, Stratton Hall	10
Mrs. Hibbert . . .	1	William King, Esq. . .	3
Mrs. Higgins . . .	10	Miss Kingsmill . .	1
Mrs. Hicks . . .	3		
Mrs. Herrieff . . .	4	Rev. John Lane . .	5
J. T. Hedges, Esq. . .	1	Mrs. Lane . . .	6
James T. Hodgson, Esq. .	1	Mrs. William Lawrence .	1
Walter Holbech, Esq. .	1	O. W. Lang, Esq. . .	1

	Copies		Copies
Miss Lay . . .	2	Mrs. Mitchell, of Standen	
Mrs. Litchfield . .	2	Hussey . . .	5
Mrs. Lightfoot . .	1	Mrs. Mitchell . . .	1
Miss Lascelles . . .	1	Mrs. John Mitchell . .	5
Miss Lewis . . .	1	Mrs. Miller . . .	1
Miss Sarah Lewis . .	1	Mrs. Milligan . . .	2
Mrs. Langcombe . .	1	Mrs. Maberley . .	2
Mrs. John Llewelyn . .	1	Mrs. McNeill . . .	1
Richard Lee, Esq. . .	1	Foster Melliar, Esq. .	2
Mrs. Lee	1	Mrs. Foster Melliar . .	2
Miss Georgiana Lee . .	1	Chas. P. Morewood, Esq.	2
Mrs. Leighton . .	1	Miss Palmer Morewood .	1
Mademoiselle Lenoir .	2	Mrs. Fred. P. Morewood .	1
Mrs. Lockwood . .	5	Miss Molyneux . .	1
Mrs. London . .	12	Robert Morritt, Esq. .	2
Miss London . .	8	Miss Miles . . .	3
Mrs. Barneby Lutley .	1	Mrs. McGildowny . .	1
Mrs. Alfred Lawrence .	1	Miss Scott Murray . .	1
Col. Little . . .	1	Miss Mulligan . . .	3
Mrs. Little . . .	1	Mrs. Morrell . . .	1
Mrs. Luff . . .	1		
Rev. J. Lys . . .	1	Rev. Canon Nepean .	2
		Miss Nepean . . .	6
James Matherson, Esq. .	5	Miss Annie E. Nepean .	1
E. H. Marshall, Esq. .	1	Miss Neal . . .	1
— Martin, Esq. . .	5	Henry Nethercote, Esq. .	1
T. Chester Master, Esq. .	1	Mrs. Henry Nethercote .	1
Mrs. Master . . .	1	Miss Nethercote . .	1
Chester Master, Esq., Junr.	1	Mrs. Ness . . .	1
Mrs. Augustus Master .	1	Miss Ness . . .	1
John Dorien Magens, Esq.	2	Miss Nixon . . .	1
Mrs. Wykeham Martin .	1	Mrs. Norton . . .	1
Miss Martin . . .	1	George S. Nesfield, Esq. .	1
Miss Mansfield . .	1	Mrs. Norris, of C. C. C.,	
Mrs. Olivier Massey . .	1	Oxford . . .	1
Miss H. V. Mansfield .	3	Rev. W. Foxley and Mrs.	
Alex. C. Macauley, Esq. .	2	Norris . . .	2
Mrs. Maggee . . .	1	J. Narracott, Esq. . .	2
Mrs. Mann . . .	1		
Mrs. Maxwell . . .	2	Mrs. O'Brien . . .	2
Mrs. Menzies . . .	1	Miss Onslow . . .	2
Miss Meyrick . . .	1	Rev. B. G. Onslow . .	1

	Copies
Mrs. Onslow . . .	1
Mrs. Orme . . .	1
Mrs. Osborne . . .	10
Mrs. O'Rorke . . .	1
Mrs. Olding . . .	1
J. Oxley, Esq. . .	3
Mrs. Oxley . . .	2
Mrs. J. J. Paget . .	5
Mrs. Alfred Parr . .	1
Miss Penelope . .	1
Thomas Palmer, Esq. .	2
James Peacock, Esq. .	6
Mrs. Horseley Palmer .	3
Mrs. Peel . . .	10
Charles Paris, Esq. . .	10
James Parker, Esq. . .	2
Miss Percy . . .	1
Rev. Joseph Pitt . .	2
Mrs. Pitt . . .	2
Miss Plumptre . .	1
Miss M. Plumptre . .	1
Mrs. Henry Payne . .	1
Mrs. Pipon . . .	1
Rev. J. Leybourne-Popham	1
Mrs. J. Leybourne-Popham	1
Richard Potter, Esq. .	2
Mrs. Potter . . .	1
Rev. W. H. Price . .	2
Mrs. Price . . .	1
Miss Julia Ponsonby .	1
T. Peters, Esq. . .	6
Mrs. Ramsay . . .	1
Mrs. Beville Ramsay .	1
Edward Ramsay, Esq. .	6
Chas. Reade, Esq., D.C.L.	5
Mrs. Crewe-Read . .	1
Rev. C. Risley . .	5
Holford Cotton Risley, Esq.	5
Rev. Robert Risley . .	2
Mrs. C. Spencer Ricketts	2

	Copies
Mrs. C. Rivay . . .	3
Mrs. Riddell . . .	1
Andrew Robertson, Esq. .	1
Miss Robertson . .	1
William Robertson, Esq. .	1
Mrs. Robbins . . .	1
John Rolls, Esq. . .	1
Mrs. Rolls . . .	1
Miss Georgiana Rolls .	1
Mrs. Rocke . . .	1
B. Robinson, Esq. . .	6
Mrs. Robinson . .	6
Miss Robinson . .	1
Miss Thereza Robinson .	2
G. Rolleston, Esq., M.D.,	
Professor of Anatomy .	2
Mrs. Robert Rolles . .	1
Mrs. Rogers . . .	1
Mrs. Reeve . . .	2
Alfred Rush, Esq. . .	1
Mrs. Alfred Rush . .	1
Miss Russell . . .	1
Miss Roffey . . .	1
E. O. Roumien, Esq. .	1
J. Priestly Salisbury, Esq.	2
Mrs. Sandeman . .	4
Miss Sandeman . .	4
Mrs. Georgiana Sandeman	5
Robert Sawyer, Esq. .	1
Major Say . . .	2
Mrs. Seward . . .	1
Mrs. Arthur Seawell .	1
Joseph D'A. Saunda, Esq.	1
H. F. Shebbeare, Esq. .	1
Mrs. Scott . . .	1
Miss Scriven . . .	1
Mrs. Severne . . .	1
Mrs. Severne of Wallop .	1
Mrs. Scott, Balliol College	1
Bridgeman Simpson, Esq.	1
Mrs. Sherston . . .	2

	Copies		Copies
C. Sharpe, Esq.	6	Mrs. Tait	1
J. Shaw, Esq.	1	Miss Talbot	1
Mrs. Shaw	1	A. B. Taylor, Esq.	1
Mrs. Shergold	3	J. G. Taylor, Esq.	1
Mrs. Smith, of Filkins	2	Mrs. Taylor	1
Mrs. Smith	3	Mrs. Tempest	1
Col. FitzRoy Somerset	1	Mrs. Terrot	2
Miss Shelley	1	Mrs. Tavern	1
William Stewart, Esq.	1	Miss Tilghman	1
Mrs. Stewart	1	Mrs. Tompson	1
Miss Smith	1	Miss Tompson	1
Mrs. Stratton	1	Major Green Thompson	6
Miss Street	1	Mrs. Thomas	1
Lieut.-Col. Strong	6	Mrs. Thoroton	1
Rev. Charles Edw. Strong	1	Mrs. Thorpe	2
Mrs. William Strong	1	Mrs. Tooth	6
Miss Clare Strong	1	Col. Le Poer Trench	1
Miss Julia Strong	2	Miss Le Poer Trench	1
Mrs. Sparke	1	Frederick Le Poer Trench	1
Rev. E. Stephenson	1	Richard Twiss, Esq.	1
Mrs. Sandeman	1	Edward Trinder, Esq.	1
Miss Sparke	1	Mrs. Edward Twisden	2
Mrs. Sharpe	1	Samuel Twining, Esq.	3
Mrs. St. Leger	6	Mrs. Twining	3
Mrs. Staddon	5		
Rev. Richard Stephens	3	Madame Uzielli	5
Mrs. Stephens	3	Mrs. Vaughan	1
Mrs. Stephens	2		
Rev. S. Symons	2	Col. Wallington	1
Mrs. Stevens	2	Mrs. Wallington	1
H. Symons, Esq.	1	Mrs. Wade	1
Capt. Stanhope, R.N.	1	Miss Waller, of Farming-	
Mrs. Spiers	3	ton Grove	1
Mrs. Stevenson	1	Mrs. Ernest Waller	1
Mrs. Slocock	1	C. H. Ward, Esq.	1
Mrs. Symonds	2	Miss Walker	1
Miss Symonds	1	Miss Ward	1
Mrs. Summers	12	Mrs. Watkins	3
Mrs. Sutton, of Benham		Edmund White, Esq.	1
Park	10	Mrs. Edmund White	2
Miss Sutton	3	Miss White	1
Rev. M. R. Scott	1	Col. Whimper	1

	Copies		Copies
Mrs. Whimper	1	Mrs. Wharton Wilson	1
Capt. G. Weir	5	J. Whippy, Esq.	4
Mrs. James Weir	2	Halifax Wyatt, Esq.	1
Miss Weir	6	Rev. C. L. Wingfield	1
Colonel Wigram	1	Miss Winter	2
Mrs. C. Wyndham	1	Miss Williams	1
Frederick Willer, Esq.	1	Miss T. Williams	1
Miss Wickes	1	Master Herbert Williams	1
Mrs. Willes	2	Master Barnard Williams	1
Miss Willes	2	Mrs. Adolphus White	1
Mademoiselle Widmer	1	Wenman Wykeham, Esq.	1
Charles Willes, Esq.	1	Mrs. Wood	1
Mrs. Charles Willes	1	Mrs. Heathcote Wyndham	1
Mrs. Walker	1	Mrs. Henry Woodhouse	3
T. F. Woods, Esq.	1	H. G. White, Esq.	3
Mrs. Woods	1		
Miss Woods	1	Miss Young	1
Wharton Wilson, Esq.	1	Miss Annie Young	1

Parishioners of Rendcomb, Gloucestershire.

	Copies		Copies
Mrs. W. Barradale	1	Mr. Stephen Price	1
Mrs. Bliss	1	Mrs. Stephen Price	1
Mrs. John Burrows	1	Mrs. Sparks	1
Miss Hester Gegg	1	Mrs. Tarrant	1
Mr. Kirby	1	Mrs. Taylor	1
Mrs. Kirby	1	Mrs. D. Taylor	1
Miss Moss	1	Miss Terry	1
Mrs. Munday	1	Mrs. Wikendon	1
Mr. Price	1	Miss Wright	1

PRINTED BY JAMES PARKER AND CO., CROWN-YARD, OXFORD.